Th

And C ˙˙˙ ˙˙ ˙ales

PAUL J KEARNS

i

ISBN: 1979632464
ISBN-13: 978 1979632461

ii

FOR CARRIE, QUINN AND ERIN

CONTENTS:
SEVEN TWISTED TALES

ACKNOWLEDGMENTS

Thank you to Carrie for supporting me through this and giving me the much needed kick up the bum to get my writing published.

Thank you to my Mum and Dad for bringing me up right, teaching me to never give up, teaching me that I can shape my own future, that if I want something to go out and get it, and not to just expect it to be handed to me on a plate.

Thank you to my brother, Noel, for teaching me to stick up for myself and being a big brother and a friend.

Thank you to my sister-in law, Sam, for being awesome.

Thank you to all my family for being there when we needed you and for being amazing.

Thank you to my friends, you know who you are and you know I love you all.

Thank you too all my followers on all social media sites.

Thank you to CreateSpace and Amazon.

Thank you to Louise Croft for proofreading.

Thank you to Lena Hedges www.forayintofashion.com for editing.

Thank you to Alex Aspinall www.facebook.com/beardedapecreative for creating the front cover.

This book is the second edition of
The Hunted and other twisted tales.
The first was published 2nd October 2016

THE HUNTED

One bullet was all that it took to seal Michael's fate and eventually cause his death, one bullet shot into the head of the wrong man. It was an accident and done in self-defence. Jake had been trying to kill him. He had come at him with a stake and an ultra violet torch with which he had burned Michael's face and chest. He had then kicked Michael while he was on the floor and turned him over ready to plunge the stake through his heart.

Michael was only a young vampire but in his human life he had been a thirty-five year old police officer and a skilled marksman. He had just reacted, pulled his sidearm and fired; but as they say practice makes perfect.

The bullet in question had passed right between Jake's eyes and killed him in an instant. It wouldn't have been so bad if Jake was a human, but he wasn't just a human. He was Jake McIntyre, the first son of Jahlob McIntyre, one of the founding members of the Wolven

2

clans. Now he lay dead here on the floor of this old dance hall. He was eight hundred and twenty years old and born a werewolf; now he was dead at the hands of a bitten vampire.

Sapora grabbed Michael, threw him over her shoulder and ran. She didn't have time for a car, she just ran as fast as she could across the rooftops. They are a great way to travel when you don't want to draw attention from humans in the streets.

She had once been caught by a speed camera running at ninety eight miles per hour. The photo had been deemed a mistake by the police and rejected. Strangely, it had disappeared from their files and was now proudly pinned to the wall in her quarters.

Sapora was three hundred years old when she had turned Michael into a vampire. She had been watching him for days while scouting for new skilled recruits.

The day she turned him he had been chasing a man who had robbed a convenience store. The man had shot wildly behind him and managed to hit

Michael in the chest and neck. Sapora found him dying and knew that this was the last opportunity she would have to turn him. She had saved him and given him his new life as a vampire. That had been five years ago.

Thanks to modern technology the news of Jake's death had already reached the bunker by the time they arrived.

Boltat was waiting for them inside, his teeth were clamped tightly together as they always were when he was angry. He was a strange looking vampire, some said he was four thousand years old. Time had ravaged him and he was big, nearly eight feet tall. His skin was like leather with hard horn like protrusions running down the middle of his head in a row like a Mohawk and he liked to tell stories of how he was the first American vampire.

"You bring a great danger to our door young one," said Boltat.

"With respect elder, The Wolven one was trying to kill him," said Sapora.

"You could have ran, Sapora."

"Please Lord. Jake had Michael on the floor, he acted in self-defence."

4

"I understand he was in human form with it not being a full moon till tomorrow night."

"Yes lord, but..."

"No but," cut in Boltat. "He was at his most vulnerable. We all know that when one of the Wolven is still in their human form they can be killed as easily as a mere human."

"Look at my face. Look at my body," said Michael ripping open his shirt. "He was trying to kill me, I defended myself."

"I know, Michael, you are young but you must understand we have laws for good reason. We have held a peace with the Wolven clans for centuries by keeping within those laws. I trust you know these laws?" said Boltat. Michael bowed his head.

"Yes my Lord."

"And what does the law state when it comes to killing of a werewolf?"

"A vampire can only kill a werewolf when they are taken by the beast form under the power of the moon," Michael recited.

"There is a reason for this law, young Michael. If we killed them when they were in their human form there would be none of their species left. We can change at any time, they cannot. The Wolven law on killing vampires states: 'A werewolf can only kill a vampire when they are awoken from slumber under the power of the moon,' for the same reason."

"But in their beast form they are monstrous compared to us. They could come and defeat us whenever they liked," protested Michael.

"But they do not, Michael. That is because the law prevents it."

"But they could say fuck the laws and wipe us out tomorrow…"

"That is enough!" said Boltat as he stood up from his throne. "Jahlob is extremely angry that his son is dead. Even more so as his death comes at the hands of such a young vampire; a bitten vampire may I add. If I do not act now your actions could throw the fragile peace we have with the Wolven into chaos. To appease his anger Jahlob said he wants you."

"He wants me?" said Michael.

"The law states that he can request a

meeting with those responsible for the death of his kin. He has made such a request and I have obliged," said Boltat.

"I'm so sorry, Michael," said Sapora.

"The request was for *both* of you!" thundered Boltat, the veins bulged in his neck.

"But I didn't kill him," snapped Sapora.

"That is circumstantial," said Boltat.

"This is bullshit! I request an appeal," she said.

"Your request is denied. You will both be cast out of the vampire Empire," he continued ignoring her protests. "None can aid these two once they leave this safe house at the penalty of death. You are exiled forthwith into the hands of the Wolven. This is in keeping with the laws set down by our Vampire Lord Ruhsarr Miehyelzah and Grand Alpha Chief of the Wolven Lords Valder McKernnan. This ruling is final. Do you have any last words?"

"This is a death sentence!" said Sapora.

"This is the law," said Boltat.

"In that case, with the highest respect

possible my Lord, go fuck yourself," said Sapora.

"What the hell? You're kicking us out, just like that?" said Michael.

"Take them away!" said Boltat.

"Fuck you too then you ugly old fuck!" said Michael.

Michael and Sapora were thrown out of the bunker with whatever they had arrived with. Sapora's friend managed to hand her a small bag of ammunition on the way out. The thick, steel doors were shut and locked behind them.

"What now?" said Michael.

Sapora stared at him, her Spanish eyes were like knives ready to cut his heart out.

"Fucking asshole. I chose you because I thought you would be a good vampire, now we're both fucked!" she said, her voice broke into a scream.

"It's not my fault. He was trying to kill me. He would have killed me if I hadn't shot him!" Michael snapped back.

"Agghh! You stupid fuck, you should have let him! I should have killed you for him!"

"Fuck you, Sapora, I wasn't just

gonna lie there and let a fucking wolf kill me. It was self-preservation, kill or be killed!"

She stared at him. Her eyes burning with killer intent. She closed them, took a deep breath and when she opened them the anger was gone. In its place was centuries of training.

"Right, ok, this isn't helping. We need to get to the car, there are guns in the trunk, and blades too. We need to move, the sun will be up in an hour and a half. We need somewhere to hide so we can to be ready for what happens tomorrow night. I don't know when Jahlob will get into New York."

"What will he be coming for?"

"Us, he'll be coming for us."

"I know, I mean what will this meeting be about? Do we have to apologise or something?"

"Apologise? Michael, he's going to hunt and kill us!"

"Oh shit… Oh fuck! I didn't realise, Sapora, I didn't know…"

"We don't have time for this, we need to move."

They ran back into New York City where

they searched the old districts and eventually found a place to sleep in an old warehouse basement.

"I hate sleeping near humans," said Sapora.

"Right now we have no choice," said Michael.

"Uggghh, I know, I know," she said. The basement was usually a hiding place for crackheads and the homeless. Despite the smell of human urine and faeces they lay down and got as much sleep as they could.

Outside the sun burned its way across the sky and flight 3432 from Glasgow landed in New York City airport.
A middle aged, stocky man with a cataract filled left eye and greatly receding hairline walked down to the arrivals lounge. He was greeted by a tall, slender woman with long black hair who went by the name of Angie. She wore skinny, ripped jeans and a purple vest top. She had tattoos all down her right arm and up her long neck.

"Mr. McIntyre?" she said in a strong Manhattan accent.

"Hello love. Are you the welcoming

committee?"

"Yes Sir. Please accept my condolences. We're all very sorry about Jake."

They continued walking as she led him to the car.

"Thank you. I will get the bastards that did this," he said.

"How was your flight?"

"The flight was terrible as always, it was worth all the hassle though and I'm all the better for seeing you Angie. Could Valder not be here to meet me too?" he said.

She couldn't help but smile. He was a likeable man, not like Valder at all.

"No Sir, he's busy but he sent me to make sure you were comfortable."

"It's a shame, I would have liked to talk with him. Your presence more than makes up for his absence though," he said as she opened the car door and he stepped in. She shut the door, walked around to the other side and climbed in next to him.

"As of 7.30 tonight I'm here on business but you will come and have a few wee drinks with me won't you? I always like the company of a beautiful woman and some well-aged whiskey before going on a hunt."

"Of course, Sir."

"Call me Jahlob."

"Of course Jahlob. The bar is fully stocked at the house."

"In that case, back to the house please Jenkins."

"Yes Sir," said the driver and pulled away from the airport.

The spring air was sweet and they drank lots of whiskey on the lawn of the large house. Despite being in mourning Jahlob regaled Angie with stories of victories and successful hunts of the years gone by.

The day moved along at a nice pace until Jahlob looked at his watch.

"Angie, as always it has been a pleasure but alas I must leave you," he said.

"It's seven thirty already?" she said.

"I'm afraid so. I'll see you tomorrow though."

"Ok," she said breezily.

He kissed the back of her hand then Jenkins escorted him to the car and drove him to the place where his son had been killed.

He walked into the old dance hall and sniffed the air. The local werewolf pack had already moved Jake's body but there was still blood stains where he had fallen. Jahlob bent down and kneeled at the spot. Outside the sun was setting, he snorted the air and felt the change begin. He caught the distinctive scent of two vampires, a male and a female. He moved to a sitting position and closed his eyes then breathed deep and slow. The wolf spirit that he had bound to his own so many years ago raged to be released. The pain came as it began to alter his physical body, even after millennia it still hurt.

Michael and Sapora began to awake from their slumber. An old man was looking at Sapora. He took her gun and looked at it; turning it in his hands. Her eyes shot open, she grabbed his left arm but he held up the gun and pointed it at her face.

"What you gonna do now lady? I got your gun," he laughed.

Before he could think she grabbed his neck and snapped it.

"Puto idiota," she hissed as she caught her gun and dropped his lifeless body to the floor.

She looked at some of the homeless people and addicts who were taking shelter in the basement. They were all taking notice now as the old man lay in a heap. Some of them were getting to their feet.

"Can we eat these people?" Michael Whispered.

"No, some of them are intoxicated or diseased; we need to find good stock."

"We need to feed."

"We also can't afford to be impaired by anything these people may have in their blood. If this werewolf finds us we need to be in the best condition possible."

"How bad can he be? There are two of us and only one of him," laughed Michael.

"Michael, Jahlob is one of the oldest werewolves in existence. There is no telling how powerful he may be," said Sapora in a scolding tone.

They got out of the warehouse before the people in there raised the alarm, then made their way into more populated parts of the city.

A couple walking in a park were a perfect target. The vampires fed as fast as they could, there was no time to waste.

Michael just about managed keep up with Sapora as they ran across the rooftops but she was extremely fast. They stopped near the old dance hall and perched on the roof of the opposing building.

"Look, the car is still there," said Sapora.

"Yes, looks like no one has been near it," said Michael.

"I hope so, let's go," said Sapora. As she jumped off the root top Michael followed close behind. They landed silently, side by side, on the ground below then ran from shadow to shadow till they reached the car.

Sapora went to open the trunk of the car but saw that it had been forced open and was slightly ajar. She threw it open, there was ammunition and swords but no guns.

"Shit!" she said.

A deep, gruff, powerful voice came from a nearby alley in answer to Sapora's exclamation.

"Looking for these?"

They both looked in the direction the voice had come from.

An eight foot tall werewolf stood there holding four guns above his head in one clawed hand. He took hold of the other end of the weapons with his other hand and swung them down to break them over his knee. Before they made contact with his leg both Sapora and Michael drew their side arms and shot at him. Bullets hit him in the face and chest. He fell back into the alley and dropped the guns. Michael ran as fast as he could and retrieved them as Sapora grabbed the swords and ammunition from the car. A roar came from the alley. Michael ran to the car holding the guns as Jahlob came barging out of the alley way. They raised their side arms again but as they did his face seemed to bubble under the surface. His chest and shoulders heaved and grew. His ribs bulged under his flesh and his bones shifted. They crunched and popped as they repositioned themselves.

"Is he getting bigger?" whispered Michael.

Jahlob threw his growing hands in the air and slammed them down. The tarmac shattered under the impact. He let out a huge roar that seemed part anger and part pain. His legs followed the rest of his body, they trembled like he was going to lose his balance, then stretched and the muscles bulged. When his bones and muscles finally came to rest he stood fifteen feet tall and towered above them.

"I told you he's not just another wolf, Michael. In the car, now. This is crazy." Jahlob ran forward slammed both fists down onto the bonnet and flattened the engine block, he then slapped the car aside smashing it into a wall.

"Which one of you will be first then?" said Jahlob.

They looked at each other, then split up and ran.

"You know that won't help you." He called after them. "I can smell your blood." Then he let out a long, loud howl and gave chase.

Sapora ran down an alley and scaled the building to her left in one jump. She needed to find Michael, he had the guns. She ran across the rooftops and listened. She heard him breathing heavily as he crashed around inside the building below her. She ran to the roof's edge and looked down. Michael jumped through a window and ran into a courtyard. The wall of the building he had just ran out of exploded. Bricks and dust flew in every direction, Jahlob came out unscathed with dust blowing from his fur. He ran after Michael who was shooting wildly behind him as he ran. Sapora had to get down to him, she pulled one of the long blades from the bag and slung the bag back round her shoulders. She unsheathed the blade and leapt as far out as she could into the courtyard. Michael grew desperate now as he searched for an exit but was not having any luck. He found himself cornered with Jahlob striding towards him.

"Got you, you little shit," he growled in

his Scottish accent.

He swung his right arm back to claw at the tiny vampire. At that moment a weight crashed down on his left shoulder. A pain surged through him and he roared. Sapora pulled the silver blade up from his body and immediately drove back into him again. Jahlob screamed and thrashed his enormous frame around trying to grab her with his right hand but she dodged twice. The third time he got her, pulled her from his back and threw her like a rag doll. She hit the wall to the right of Michael and fell to the ground. Straight away he helped her up, they ran to the nearest door, pulled it open and ran inside. Jahlob pulled the blade from his shoulder and threw it at them, it embedded itself in the door inches behind them but they kept on running. They ran deeper into the building and could see it was an old warehouse that had been converted into office space. There were plasterboard office cubicles everywhere and they ducked into one of them.

    "Here, load the guns," Sapora said, as

she pulled the bag from her back and unzipped it.

Michael slapped a magazine into her CbS 480, (a vampire designed and built gun. It was fully automatic with recoil dampeners and an infrared laser target) cocked it and passed it to her. He pushed a 32 shot magazine into his AA12 automatic shotgun and slung it over his shoulder. He then picked up his CbS 480. By now Sapora's broken bones had shifted themselves back into place and healed.

The outside wall shook and burst apart. When the dust cleared the wolf was stooped right down and walking into the building. As he went he looked down into the cubicles, snorting at the air. Michael and Sapora were on their hands and knees scuttling away through the gaps between the cubicles.

"Fee, fi, fo, fum," growled Jahlob. He walked forward tearing apart the offices. The vampires split up and went in opposite directions.

"I smell the..."

"Silver bullets!" shouted Michael. He jumped up and let of a burst of

ammo right at Jahlob's head who in turn
roared and charged at him. A burst of
bullets hit him in the back. He spun and
looked around. The muzzle flare gave
away Sapora's location. He charged at
her. Another burst hit him in his back
and again he turned. Then another burst
hit him in his back, each time from a
different location. He turned and
snarled, he was getting tired of this
game. He put his head down and
charged on all fours in the direction of
the bullets until he hit something fleshy.
Michael was thrown from the huge head
of the beast and smashed through office
cubicles. He lay dazed for a second
then a clawed hand grabbed him by the
foot and swung him like a club. Plaster
board, desks and computers shattered
around his body then Jahlob let him go.
He smashed through a row of cubicles
then came to a stop on the floor. He was
cut, battered and bleeding so for a
moment he lay still. He could hear the
rat, tat, tat of a Sapora's gun and
Jahlob's roars of anger.
Sapora ran from Jahlob, shooting at him
as she went. He roared and thrashed,

destroying cubicles as he ran. He swung
for her and caught her ankle. She fell
and slid across the polished floor. He
swiped her up with his hand around her
waist and squeezed her till she
screamed. He laughed as she kicked
her legs and beat at his huge hand with
her fists.

"You can't get away from me missy.
Now scream," he squeezed her again
and she screamed.
Michael shook his head and stumbled to
his feet, he could hear Sapora
screaming and the deep, heavy laughter
of the werewolf. He stumbled a bit more
but held his balance. He checked his
weapons and found he had lost his CbS
480 but still had his sidearm, his knife,
his AA12 and two 32 round barrel
magazines. He ran toward Sapora's
screams.
Jahlob was holding her head to his
mouth. She was pushing back against
his snout and lower jaw with her hands,
trying to keep them from closing.
Micheal aimed at Jahlob's right ankle
and pulled the trigger twice. The blasts
of shot tore into his flesh. He roared and

swung her away from his mouth. She pulled out her sidearm and shot him four times in his mouth, tearing his tongue and shattering some teeth. He screamed and in a rage slammed her down into the floor. Michael shot him in the side three times exposing his ribs. He roared in pain, let go of Sapora and ran into the darkness. She lay on the floor coughing up blood.

"Are you ok?" Michael shouted running to her side.

"I'll live, just help me up please," she said and reached out to him. Michael pulled her to her feet and she cried out in pain. She forced herself to take a deep breath and stood up straight. Her ribs and pelvis clicked then locked back into place.

Jahlob growled somewhere from the dark to their left. They stood still and looked around. A growl came from behind them, then to their right. Michael fired a shot into the dark but Jahlob just laughed. He fired another shot and got nothing but more laughter.

"He's circling us," said Sapora. Michael fired again and this time there was a scream. They then heard him running at them so they themselves turned and ran. Jahlob's huge frame loomed behind them. Michael pointed the shotgun behind him and fired three times. Jahlob screamed, stumbled, and smashed through cubicles but kept moving. They ran through a door which lead into the reception area.

There was a front desk, a row of chairs and prints of famous paintings on the wall.

They ran and leapt over the chairs then ran down a corridor trying the doors on either side as they went. Soon they found one that wasn't locked. Inside was a conference room with a long table surrounded by chairs. Jahlob smashed through the wall from the room with office cubicles to the reception area. Michael stood in the corridor outside the conference room and fired three shots at him. Jahlob ran at the little vampire, roaring as the bullets tore at his flesh. He slammed into Michael, smashed him through the wall, he landed on the table which broke and splintered. Jahlob stepped through the hole in the wall, he

picked up a six foot piece of wood and snapped it across Michael's back. He wailed in pain while Jahlob punched and stamped on his head repeatedly as he lay on the floor. He turned Michael over onto his back. The vampire spat at him and with a blood drenched smile said,
    "Is that all you've got?"
Jahlob snarled and went to grab him with his right hand. Michael lifted the shotgun, pressed the barrel to Jahlob's palm and pulled the trigger. Blood, bone and clawed fingers flew in all directions. Jahlob's screams filled the air as he waved the bloody, torn, flesh of his wrist like a man who had hit his thumb with a hammer. Blood pumped from the savage wound. Michael sat and laughed until Jahlob kicked him hard in the face. He then grabbed Michael around the chest with his remaining hand.
    "What are you going to do now, tickle me?" said Michael.
Jahlob stood a foot on Michael's thighs and pulled him upwards. He screamed as the bones of his legs snapped one after the other. The flesh and muscles stretched, then tore. Blood spilt across

the carpet covered floor, Michael howled and passed out as the last strands of skin broke free. Jahlob held him up to his face.

"Not so much the comedian now are we," he said in a quiet sinister voice. Sapora had jumped through the window of the room onto the road outside and driven by panic she had ran for her life. She came to her senses, turned and ran back to the warehouse. As she looked through the broken window she saw the horrific scene inside, a tear rolled down her cheek and she shot wildly at the beast. Jahlob roared and threw the legless Michael her but she caught him and lay him down on the floor.

"Holy fuck...Ah shit...Michael...I...I'm so sorry," she sobbed.
At that Moment Jahlob burst through the wall. Bricks and mortar showered everything on the road including Sapora and Michael. In the chaos Micheal thrust the Shotgun into Sapora's hand and said,

"Take this. Go. I'm not getting out this time."

"But..."

"No. You've saved me more time than I deserve, now save yourself."
She kissed him on the forehead, took the gun and ran.
Jahlob shook his head and made to run after her but Michael grabbed his ankle. He pulled himself up through the fur to Jahlob's thigh and sunk his fangs into the flesh. Jahlob screamed and grabbed him but he held on like an oversized tick. He pulled, and punched Michael then using all his strength he managed to dislodge him. He pounded him with the stump of his wrist until Michael bit that too. Jahlob waved his limb around but was unable to shift Michael. Eventually he removed the vampire by holding him up to his mouth and biting off his left arm. Michael released his bite hold to half scream, half roar. Jahlob roared back then clamped his jaws around the Michael's head and bit down. He clawed at Jahlob's face with his one remaining hand and tore off his left eyelid. This only caused Jahlob to bite down harder and shake his head. Michael's skull was crushed and his flesh turned to burning ash that swirled

27

through the air. The wolf coughed and shook the remains from his mouth.

"That was for Jake," he spat more ash into the floor. "Fuck me, you tough little cunt," said Jahlob.
He then snorted at the night air.

"Senorita. Where did you get too baby?"
Sapora ran across rooftops looking for somewhere to hide. She leapt twenty feet onto the roof of another building. She could hear Jahlob as he called and howled so loud it hurt her ears. She heard him crash into the building that she ran across. The noise from the interior being torn apart got closer to her position. A hand burst up through the roof five feet in front of her. She jumped over it but as she landed her left foot broke through the roof causing her to stumble and fall. She rolled down the roof and crashed through a skylight. She hit the floor below but with all her weight and momentum she smash through that too. She hit the ground-floor and her bones cracked. She was dazed but managed to roll onto her back. Her bones locked back into place and began

to heal. She squeezed her eyes shut and tried to force the pain away. When she opened them Jahlob was standing over her.

"Hello sweetie pie," he said with grin that showed his ash covered teeth. He stamped his foot down in an attempt to crush her head. She quickly rolled out of the way into a crouched position where she pulled a three foot blade from her back and hissed at him. He took a step towards her but she swiped at him with the blade. He moved back and growled. He then lunged for her but she flipped out of the way and sliced at his right ear as she went. He landed on his front paw and spun to face in her direction. As he crouched and rested his weigh on his one good hand he looked at her, then down at the stump where his other hand would have been.

"Does it sting?" she said in a mocking tone.

"On the contrary," replied Jahlob, "It's getting better."

As she looked at his arm small finger like protrusions grew from the healed stump. They began to form a hand that then grew bigger and sprouted fur and claws.

"Live long enough and you pick up a few tricks along the way," he said as he flexed the new hand, then swiped out at her.

"How handy," she said with smirk as she jumped out of the way.
She landed and ran off through the building. He gave chase but as she disappeared round a corner he lost her, but he could still follow her scent. He slowed to a walk and sniffed at the air. He could smell her but she was hiding. He looked around inhaling long and deep. She fell silently from the ceiling onto his back, then stabbed the blade into his neck and twisted it. She pulled the blade from his neck and stabbed him in the back. His muscles were tough but the sharp blade sliced through them with ease. He screamed and shook trying to dislodge her. She jumped to the ground, slashed across his Achilles tendon and ran. He howled and roared in her direction. His ankle was bleeding but started to heal with his focused efforts. He limped in the direction she

had ran.

She needed to use the time and distance that she was putting between them wisely. She jumped through a window not bothered that he would hear the sound and in fact she needed him to hear it.

She found herself in a demolition site. 'I need something big,' she thought to herself.

She ran past all sorts of vehicles and machinery. When she saw what she was looking for her eyes lit up.

Jahlob's ankle was taking it's time to heal. Regrowing his hand after healing all the bullet and stab wounds had taken a lot out of him. He found the broken window and threw himself through the wall. He limped out into the demolition site and sniffed the night air.

He had her scent now and he followed it. It zig-zagged as if she was looking for something, probably a place to hide. The building that was being demolished was flood lit and the light caught something lay still on ground about five feet from it. He snorted the air and the scent lead right to it. He walked over to the item and scooped it up. It was just her coat. A wolf whistle pierced the air and he looked up to see Sapora sat in a mobile crane.

"Here doggie," she said.
He drew his lips back from his huge teeth and he snarled just as a wrecking ball swung down. It slammed into him and crushed him against the building. The ball swung away and jerked from side to side as it went. He slid to the floor, his body racked with pain. Just about every bone was broken, his flesh was split and ragged. His breath laboured and he drifted towards unconsciousness. He had never felt so battered and weak in his life.
She climbed down from the crane and walked over to him. He lay on his side so she rolled him onto his back and stepped up onto his chest.

"You...fuckin'...fuckin'…" he coughed.

"Bitch?" she suggested.

"Sneaky cunt!" he said finishing his sentence.

"Fucked with the wrong motherfuckers this time didn't you?" she said.

"I'm not finished yet," he hissed and swung a broken hand at her.
She swiped out with her blade the hand flew from his arm and flopped to the floor. She plunged the blade into his chest and cut open his shattered sternum. She flung the blade aside and thrust her hands into his chest. With all her might she pulled open his ribcage to reveal his heart and lungs. She took Michael's AA12 from her shoulder and pressed the barrel against his heart. She pulled the trigger until the magazine was empty. His lungs were torn to ribbons and his heart was shredded. His body began to convulse and blood flowed from his clenched jaws. Sapora jumped down from his chest. He gasped and choked as his arms and legs shrank down to their human size. His body and head jerked violently then shrank too. He thrashed his head wildly as the wolf like muzzle reverted to his human face. For a second a man lay there. He gasped for breath then his skin tightened and dried up. He looked at her as his eyes sunk into his head and disintegrated. His chest collapsed while

his fingers and toes curled up tight. His arms pulled into his chest, his legs kicked out and became rigid as the muscles pulled away from the bones. Finally three thousand years of decay caught up with Jahlob and in a matter of moments his mummified shell fell to dust.

Sapora looked at the pile of dust, put her head back and sighed. There was a movement, a swirl of wind and from the dust rose a spirit in the form of huge wolf. It looked at her right in the eyes then bowed its head in thanks. It then turned and ran out into the darkness. Sapora smiled and looked at the AA12.

"I couldn't have done it without you, Michael," she said.

She ejected the empty magazine and replaced it with a full one. There was more ammunition in the car, also a gun with a magazine somewhere in the office where they had fought Jahlob. She looked at her watch and she saw there were four hours until sunrise.

"Still some time for a little payback, Boltat." she said and made her way back to the wreck of the car.

THE RAILWAY BRIDGE

I have never uttered a word of this to anyone. Now I'm just going to write it down here and never mention it again. It was a cold night in the middle of winter. I had just withdrawn some money from a cash machine and was walking to the train station to go home. I passed under the old, dark, railway bridge. The same way I had done every day of my working life. I saw a movement from the corner of my eye. A fist hit me, I stumbled, then was pushed and I fell.

I tried to roll away but my attacker jumped on me. He pushed his big knee into my chest and pinned me. He was about forty five years old, six feet five inches and at least seventeen stone. I threw a sloppy punch and missed. He pulled out the biggest knife I have ever seen and spat his words in desperation.

"Stop fighting or I'll stick you man. I'll fucking stick you right here."

I put up my hands in submission.

"Good, now give me your money."

I was a cocky shit back then and replied,
   "I can't, it's for my brother. He will kill
me if I don't pay him."
He pressed the tip of the knife against
my throat and spoke more deliberately
now.
   "I'll kill you right here, right now, bitch.
Give me the fucking money!"
I was beat and I knew it. Many thoughts
ran through my head at that moment.
The main one being 'This is it. My ticket
is being punched right here under this
shitty, old bridge.'
The sound of something shuffled close
by. A long, slender, pale hand grabbed
him by the chin and lifted him off me like
he was a bag of feathers. I scrambled
away and pulled myself to my feet. My
legs wanted to run but I somehow
forced myself to look back. The man
was on his knees with a tall slim woman
hunched over him; her head buried in
his neck. Her body was loosely covered
by ragged old clothes and her skin was
infected with festering sores. She looked
like a meth addict.
Blood oozed down his chest. He tried to
swing the knife at her but with a swift

movement she grabbed his forearm and shook it. The bones popped out from the skin and splattered blood across his legs. She never took her face away from his neck.

I just stood there frozen, only able to shake with fear.

Slowly she lifted her head from his neck. Blood dripped from her ugly, lipless mouth. A long, snake-like, tongue ran over her long, serrated, blood soaked teeth. It was clear that she was no meth head.

"You...you...saved me," I said with a stammer.

"Yes, I did. Now run, before I change my mind," she snarled at me and her blood shot, hollow eyes turned to slithers of darkness against her pale skin.

I turned and ran. I ran like I had never run before and I didn't stop till I got home four miles away.

I am Wolf

After walking for a day and a half we are all hungry. A deer catches Running Claw's attention. Its nose twitches as it looks up at him while he is closing in on it. It makes a move as if to run but Feather Walker lunges and tears into its neck from its blind side. That is it, we all move in and bring it down fast and clean.

This food is well received and will keep us going for the next few days. When we have finished our meal we lick each other clean of the blood.

We walk a while longer. The forest here is thicker than it has been for the past day and grows in an unnatural pattern. Standing Bear, our Alpha male, smells the air then he speaks. We do not speak vocally but telepathically.

"There are humans nearby. We should be careful," he said.

Mountain Call, our Alpha Female, says:

"Yes they are not known for the tolerance of our kind."

We walk on but keep our distance. I look

through the trees and see a shopping centre. It's dawn, the sun is coming up and there is no one around except a few cars on the roads. I look up to the sky. The full moon is still visible but around it the sky is a dark blue that gets lighter with every passing moment. I can see rays of sun illuminating the clouds from beyond the horizon. The fur on my back stands on end and I can feel the change in my mind. I have felt this coming for a few days now I have to stop and rest.

"Are you ok?" asks Mountain Call.

"The Change, I feel it," I say.
I grit my teeth and giving my head a shake.

"The Change? It's been a while for you."

"Almost a year and a half. Should I not be past this by now?"

"We are all different. There is no rush," she says.
I look back over towards the shopping centre. I smell the air. Something dawns on me.

"What is it?" asks Mountain Call.

"I know this place. I lived here as a human."

We are werewolves of a sort, though a different breed to the common lycanthrope. The lunar cycle holds little sway over our metamorphosis. To start out with we do change with the full moon but as time wears on we spend less time as humans and more time as wolves until finally the change is permanent.

Standing Bear hasn't changed in almost four hundred years. It has been twelve years since he found me and bit me. He knew I would accept this gift and could survive the transformation; changing me for the better.

I have loved wolves since I was a child. I had studied them and worked with them in my career so I jumped at the chance to live as one.

Twelve years! Where has the time gone?

The first three were the worst. It was hard to get used to having the ability to transform. Having to leave the life I had built was even harder.

My body would scream to be a wolf until I could no longer deny it. It felt so good, so right. Unfortunately I had to let go of everything…and everyone.

My hands start to ache. The digits on my paws start to push out and elongate as the palm retracts. It's painful but tolerable. My front limbs start becoming arms and my humerus stretch. This does hurt.

My paws are now hands, my fingers splay out. I close my eyes and clench my jaw tight. My ribs move and pull my sternum up towards my spine; this changes the shape of my chest. I can't breathe to scream from this inescapable pain.

"Quick move him. If he starts to make noise he will draw the human's attention!" says Standing Bear.
They push me along.

"There is a hide not far from here. Just over the hill," says Fighting Sun. We get to the hide that is for bird watching. It provides us with shelter and camouflage.

My lungs call out for air. The muscles in my chest answer and pull in as much air as I can take. I scream it all back out then inhale deeply again. My pelvis opens out and pushes my hips apart.

My femurs grow and lengthen as the muscles stretch. I let out a howl that morphs into a scream. My feet widen as they become shorter and my digits become toes. The claws fall off leaving nails in their place. I stand up on my fur covered human legs. My back arches as I throw my head back and roar. My tail shrinks to non-existence. I now look like a wolfman. Now my head starts to change. This is without doubt the most painful part. My cranium starts to expand as my cerebral cortex returns to its human size. My wolf teeth sink back down into my gums and the human teeth slide back up into their places. The bones of my face click and shift. The forehead sliding up above my eyes and my nasal cavity and maxillary jaw slides in below them. My mandibular jaw grows down and wider and shrinks back and fits under the upper jaw. My cheekbones widen and expand around my eye sockets as my brow furrows over them. All the time I hear a man screaming in my head, I then realise it's my voice bursting from my throat. My eyes change from golden to dark brown.

The pain subsides and I'm itchy all over. I brush my hands over my brown skin knocking away the wolf fur and my transformation is complete.

I look down at my body. It has been so long since I have seen it I have almost forgotten what I look like as a human. My muscles bulge and twist under my skin as I move my limbs. I'm in good shape. When I was just human I carried a little extra weight. Without snacks or junk food but with all the exercise that comes with being a wolf I'm lean and well built. My hair and beard are longer than they were last time I changed.

I search the hide for some clean, dry clothes. I find some and put them on. The faded jeans are too large around the waist, lucky for me they have a leather belt still threaded through the belt loops. The t-shirt is far too big also. It's red and has a picture of Pink Floyd on the front. I no longer understand a human's problem with nudity but I can't go walking around naked.

"I've been thinking, I want to spend my time as a human in their world. I know this place, I used to live here. I want to see how it's changed. I will only be human till the sun sets and I don't know when or if I'll ever change again," I say.

"No, Sky Roar, you must stay with us. You are vulnerable now," says Standing Bear.

"Please, Standing Bear, My Alpha. I'll return when I turn again. I just need to do this."

"Let him go. Like he says, he might never get another chance. He is a wolf, no matter what form he's in he'll be able to defend himself," says Mountain Call. Standing Bear looks at her and she looks back at him with her soft eyes. He lets out a sigh, looks at me and says,

"Ok, but be careful. You are a wolf as Mountain Call says. You must return when you change back to your wolf form. Humans have strange ways and kill for fun. They are a dangerous breed."

"I will. Thank you Standing Bear." I find a pair of walking boots. They are too big but I tie the laces tight to stop them sliding about too much.
I walk back to the shopping centre.

There are some cars in the carpark now and some of the lights have been switched on inside the building. I run down the small embankment and quickly leap over the six foot fence.
I have another reason for wanting to come back here. Her name is Jessica. More cars start to arrive. As casually as I can, I walk towards the doors on the shopping centre. As I presumed they are locked and they bang loudly in their frame.

"We're not open yet hon. We open at ten," says a woman who's inside. She's wearing a blue t-shirt with the shopping centre logo on it.
I open my mouth to speak and realise I've not spoken vocally since I last changed. I have howled, growled, whined and whimpered but not spoken. I force out the words.

"O-o-k. Sorry."
My voice is thin and croaky. I walk away, and as I do I see the high street. The old arcade is still here. The lights are off or broken and the place looks dingier than I remember it. I continue past shops that are boarded up. There

47

used to be a cinema but now it's been turned into coffee, charity and budget shops. I spend a few hours wandering around reminiscing about the places me and Jessica used to go. There is 'The Little Italy' restaurant, the mall and 'The Loudness' rock bar. I find myself in the town centre. The town hall clock used to tower above all the other buildings. Now there are a handful of tall office buildings. Not exactly skyscrapers but still taller than the town hall. I look at the clock. I've not read a clock for so long that I have to count the numbers first. It's half past ten.

I wander into the supermarket. I'm drawn by the smell of the meat. My sense of smell is not quite lupine but is a lot more sensitive than that of a human. People are looking at me in a funny way and giving me a wide berth. The music agitates my ears and the bright colours annoy me. I have to blink a lot and hold my hands over my ears.

Eventually I find the meat aisle. I can smell the meat through the plastic packaging. It's been packed fresh but to me I can already smell the putrefaction setting in. It turns my stomach. It's edible but I'm used to the meat straight from the animal. It's the same with the fruit and vegetables. I can smell the chemicals used to make them stay fresh for longer. They are undetectable to humans but I realise that I'm more wolf than human now. I notice that a security guard is following me.

"Look, Buddy, you can't be in here if you're not going to buy anything," he says as he places a hand on my shoulder.

"I need to use the bathroom," I say.

"Ok. You can use to amenities but then be on your way."

I nod and go to men's room. I look at myself in the mirror. My hair is long, down to my shoulders and my beard makes me look like a castaway.

I come out and the security guard is waiting for me. He must think that I'm homeless. He escorts me to the door and again I'm left wandering around. It's around mid-day.

I come to a road that I remember better than the others. I feel something in my chest I have not felt for a long time, hesitation. Hell, I barely ever felt it as human; I am so impulsive. I make myself take a step forward and move slowly along the pavement. The pangs of regret and the heartbreak I had when I walked away from her sweep back over me. It's like being soaked with cold water. I try to hold back as the house comes into view. My lips tremble, the sting of tears fills my eyes, and my breath comes in stifled spasms. I can't stop myself and I weep openly. I must look weird, a full grown, scruffy man stood in the street crying. I get closer and study the house. We lived here together for five years.

We had first met in college many years before. Our relationship was wonderful and when we graduated and got jobs we moved in here together.

The memories come flooding back. The day we moved in, having parties, and making love. Even the silly little arguments that were quickly resolved come back. I loved her then, part of me still loves her now. The way she used to look at me, the way she made me feel about her and about myself. The way she used to talk. Her voice getting higher and faster when she was excited to the point her sentences would fall apart. She was amazing, so amazing, but I had to leave. How could I not? What would she do? Keep me as a pet in the back yard? Again I know I'm not human anymore. This isn't where I live, this isn't who I am. I'm a wolf in man's clothing. I need to leave this place behind so I walk away and leave the house in the past where it should stay. The day ebbs away as I walk in the park. It's hardly changed. An old couple feed the ducks as students sit on a bench and laugh about the latest TV show. I don't miss TV, nor computers. I don't understand them anymore. My world is the pack and the hunt.

I meander around the town till the sun begins its descent towards the horizon. Without warning I catch a scent on the air. It awakens my nostrils. It's a scent I hadn't smelt for a long time. It tugs at my memory.

There she is, walking right towards me. She still lives here but she looks older and has longer hair now. Her dark skin

51

shines in the light from the setting sun. She is still beautiful. She is holding hands with a man and is pushing a pushchair. I don't know what to do with myself. Do I keep going and hope they don't notice me or do I turn and run the other way?

Suddenly a man runs past, steals her handbag and runs past me too.

"My bag! My bag!" she calls out.

My instincts kick in and I'm on the hunt. I give chase and run down the busy street. I'm aware that her man is chasing too. I leap at the thief and land on his back knocking him to the floor. I try to retrieve the bag but he rolls over and punches me right on the nose. Water fills my eyes and for a moment I can't see. He's up and running.

"Thanks pal," says her man as her runs past me.

My eyes clear and the hunt is back on. I see her man catch up with the thief and push him. The thief stumbles and trips but somehow stays up. He turns and I see the glint of a knife. He slashes the air as Jessica's partner jumps back. I run at the thief and just as I get close to him he thrusts the knife forwards. I take it in the stomach. He looks at me in surprise and I look back at him the same way. His expression twists to anger as he pulls it out. It takes all my effort not to bite him. I feel my fist instinctively punch him three times and he slumps back unconscious against a shop door. As the anger in me subsides I notice he has blood coming from his nose. I bend down to him and move him into the recovery position. I take the bag and pass it to Jessica's man.

"Thank you so much, buddy," he says, panting for breath.

"No problem," I say.

"Oh man. You're bleeding," he says. I look down and there is blood soaking into the t-shirt.

"We have to get you to a hospital," he says pulling out his phone and starts dialing.

"No, it's ok. I'll be fine," I say, pleading.

"It's the least I can do," he replies. I pull up my shirt and there is little more than a deep graze.

"It's just a scratch. He hardly marked

me," I say.

"Wow. You're lucky. I could have sworn he stabbed you. I'll call the police to arrest him. You don't mind talking to the police do you?" he says.

"No, not at all," I say.

He calls the local police station and talks to the Sheriff.

Jessica is getting close but so is the change. I will be a wolf within the hour.

"He'll be here in ten minutes."

Jessica is right in front of me now.

"Thank you so much. You're so brave," she says in her beautiful voice and hugs me.

"It was nothing Ma'am. Just acting on instinct. It was the right thing to do," I say.

She looks at me for second then says,

"This may sound weird but do I know you?"

I want say yes. I want to tell her who I am, explain why I had to leave and how sorry I am. I want to hold her, to kiss her, to tell her I never forgot her and never stopped thinking about her but I can't. It would be wrong. I look at her with her man, her child and her life. A life that she has built without me. I would just be destroying her world. So I just say,

"Sorry Ma'am. You must have me mistaken for someone else."

She looks at me and smiles.

"Sorry. You just seem familiar."

"I get that all the time. I guess I just have one of those faces."

The Sheriff arrives and takes our statements. He arrests the thief and I'm congratulated many times.

We're now stood around, Jessica and her man are talking to some locals. The moon is showing through the clouds. My hands start to change. I sneak away and run into the forest. They look round but can't see me. The change is coming faster than I expected. My head is changing but I keep moving. I come to a clearing as my chest finishes changing. I howl for my pack. One by one they appear in the clearing, they have been tracking me. I look back to where Jessica is stood looking confused. I look at my pack then back to her. I know now that she is part of the human world. A world I left behind.

She is human.

I am wolf.

Standing Bear walks over to me.

"How do you feel?" he says.

"I'm good," I reply.

"Have you seen all you needed to see?" he says.

"Yes, my Alpha," I say.

"It's time to go, Sky Roar."

"Yes, it is."

We all turn and run back into the forest, back to our lives.

THE ESCAPIST

I'm gonna tell you about how I came to be living in Canada.

It was 1949, New York. Four years after the Second World War. I remember it well, how could I ever forget.

I had just run back to my apartment after Benny Goosdus told me that Mickey 'The Hammer' was looking for me. Some piece o' shit had told him where I was hiding out.

I locked the apartment door and was fumbling with the keys for my little wall safe. It wasn't big but it was strong. I slid the key into the slot, put in the combination with the number wheel and turned the key.

There inside the safe sat the little, velvet, drawstring bag. Next to it lay my gun, a Colt M1911.

I picked up the bag and just to make sure they hadn't run off in the night I had a little peep inside. They were all still there and pretty as ever.

You see I was a thief, but as a kid I was sent to live in an orphanage at the age of four. The nuns there told me my mother and father had died in a car crash. Long story short I got an education of sorts but fell in with a bad crowd.

I scraped by until Mickey 'The Hammer' recruited me for my light fingered skills. Now twenty two, I was an accomplished bank robber, with twelve robberies under my belt.

The last of which had gone sour. Johnny and Frank had been killed by the cops but I had escaped with the goods.

   I pulled the drawstrings, closing the bag and slid it into my trouser pocket. I took my gun and slid it into my side holster. I went to my bedroom and started packing. I had thrown a bunch of clothes into my case and was sifting through my ID papers when there was a knock on the door. It wasn't a nice knock either. I don't know if a knock can sound mean but, you know, that night it could have been my sweet old grandmother with a box of kittens and right at that moment it would have sounded shifty.

   "Bobby? Bobby? Come on, open the door. We knows you're in there. The boss wants a little chat with you," came the heavy New York accented voice of Donny Wisoutski.

"Yea. Come on Bobby. Don't make things any harder than they have to be. Just give the boss back the bag of jewels and everything will be straight between you and him." That was the voice of Pauli, Donny's twin brother. They were ugliest pair of motherfuckers you could ever wish to see. Even more so since they had taken up boxing.

"That ain't gonna happen," I said. There was no point lying that I didn't have the diamonds. If they got in here they would find me with them and I would have got it even worse.

Mickey wouldn't just give me beating. He probably would have used his favorite hammer on my dumb skull. Then I would have been buried in a shallow grave without so much as a tarp wrapped around me.

Mickey was a psychopath in every sense of the word.

I once had to dig the grave of a crazy prick who had dared to fuck his wife, Mary. She was drawn to Mickey's power and money but not him. He wasn't much in the way of looks. Anyways, he had found this guy in bed with her and went crazy. Even crazier than normal. He rung a few of the guys and told us to get to his house as fast as we could. It was two in the morning by the time I got there and they were in the basement. Mickey had tied this guy to a chair and had smashed his fingers to mush with a lump hammer. Mary had been tied to a chair facing her lover and was forced to watch.

"Just tell me to stop!" Mickey kept shouting at her.

But it's pretty impossible to speak, let alone say stop, when your lips are sewn shut. All Mickey's handy work. So then he takes a knife and cuts off what is left of this poor guy's hands. He then slices off his dick and balls and puts them all in a blender. The guy was screaming and crying, then Mickey forced a funnel down this guy's throat and made him drink his own hand and dick smoothie. I swear there was a look of relief on the guy's face when Mickey finally cracked his idiot skull wide open.

Mary wasn't allowed out of his sights after that. He used to lock her in the basement tied to the same blood stained chair for days on end.
That's how he treated the woman he loved. So you understand he wasn't gonna treat some little shit who 'stole' from him like a returning hero. Stole from him! The fat fuck never even lifted a finger and I stole it from the bank anyways. They never even belonged to him in the first fuckin' place.

   So yeah, anyhow. Donny and Pauli were banging on the door and the thing began to give way. This is when I started to feel that tingling in my back. Back then it was still kinda new to me but now I know the feeling well. I held up my Colt and squeezed off a round right through the door above their heads. I heard a scream and remembered the ugly brothers are about 6'5".

   "What da fuck are you doin' Bobby? You fuckin' shot me," screamed Donny. He started really beating at that door. I tore off my shirt just as the two long arm-like appendages burst through the skin and pushed out from my back.

Sounds painful, eh? That's because it fuckin' is. Not as painful as what lay in store for me otherwise, but painful all the same.

Spiny scales push outwards from the skin all over the arms. They then burst open into amazing white feathers. This is how I was able to escape from the bank.

The door splintered open all over the place and Donny came running in. Blood pouring from his ear that was half missing. By this point I was at the window. Donny ran at me screaming incoherent babble. I slid the window up and leapt out. He nearly followed me, though the one hundred foot drop was enough to make anyone change their minds. I flapped my wings and flew out across the New York skyline. Pauli pulled Donny aside and shot a few rounds none of which even came close.

They must have told someone what they saw that night, they must have done. But even if they had I doubt anyone would have believed them anyway.

That night I flew over the border to

Canada and began my new life. I sold the diamonds and made two million dollars. To keep anyone from sniffing around I opened a few different accounts, then I just moved around and kept myself to myself.

A few months later the twins were found dead. Mickey's trademark smashed skulls showed the nature of their passing.

Apparently, he never stopped looking for me.

Ten years after I left he was found dead outside his house in the suburbs. He had died from a fall. His head was smashed in and his pelvis was just under his heart. The papers said it was as if he had fallen off a skyscraper. Funny thing is all the houses around there were only two floors high. But I...er...I wouldn't know anything about that...would I?

IN THE BASEMENT

John Harper sat in the driver's seat of the blue Ford Focus. Tony Barnes was in the passenger seat and Danny Walker was in the backseat.
It was 10pm, they were watching the house of Charles Lloyd and his family. John's phone rang just as he was expecting it to and he answered.

"Hello Jack... Yes we're sat outside the house now... Yes they're all home now... Are you ready there?… Yes we're ready. We've been sat here for two fucking hours. Yes we're fucking ready... Ok, ok, Jack... Jack I'm sorry. I'm just a little tense. We've been sat here a while. I didn't mean any disrespect... Ok… Thanks Jack. I'm sorry... Yeah we've got the guns... Well yeah they're loaded but... No, no we ain't gonna shoot nobody... Yep. No, we just want to scare them really… We don't want to wake the neighbours... Yeah I know the plan Jack. Get in, tie em up, Get the code out of him and get out... Yes… Yes. Ok… Ha ha... Yeah... See you when we're

rich men."
John ended the call and turned to Tony
and Danny.

"Ok Guys this is it. Don't shoot nobody
remember, just beat them up a bit if we
have to. Mostly just tie them up and
scare them. Most of all don't shoot him.
We need the code out of him then we tie
him up and get the fuck out of here."

"Ok man," said Danny.

"Yep," said Tony.
They all checked their guns then
stepped out of the car and walked to the
front door of the house. John rang the
doorbell and they all put on their
balaclavas. Charles opened the door.

"Hello? How can…What the hell?!"
John pushed the barrel of his Smith and
Weston snub nose into Charles' right
cheek and said,

"Get inside. Don't make a scene or I'll
blow your fucking head off."
Charles walked backwards into the
house. The three men pushed their way
in and closed the door behind them.

"Charles? Who is it hun?" said his wife
Anna.
Tony pointed a sawn off shot gun at her,

"Get on the floor face down unless you want a face full of lead," he snarled.
She screamed as Tony ran over to her. He pointed the gun in her face and said,
"Get. The. Fuck. down."
She got down to the floor without any more hesitation and sobbed.
"Ok Charles Lloyd. Where is your son?" said John.
"He…he's upstairs," said Charles.
"Would you mind shouting to him and telling him to get down here."
"Now?"
"No, next fucking week. Yes fucking right now!" said John.
"Mike. Mike. Would you mind coming down here now please?" Charles shouted up the stairs.
There was some shuffling and banging and then Mike walked to the top of the stairs.
"Ugh. What have I done now?" John answered
"You won the lottery kid. Get your fucking arse down here or I'm gonna shoot your dad in the face."
Mike hurried down the stairs where Danny smacked him in the jaw with the

butt of his gun. Mike hit the floor like a sack of potatoes. Danny rolled him over onto his front and began to duct tape his hands behind his back.

"Mike! Mike! Oh God! Mike!" cried Anna.

"Tony, Tie her up too and tape her God damn mouth shut too. Her crying is getting on my fucking nerves and she's gonna alert the neighbours," said John. With that Tony pulled out a roll of tape. He grabbed her hands and taped them together. He taped her ankles in the same way. He then put her ankles to her hands and taped them together so she was hogtied. He pulled her up into a kneeling position, stuck the end of the tape over her mouth and then wrapped it around her head several times. Danny tied Mike up in the same way.

"Ok Charles. As you can see we're in control here. Now, I don't want to hurt you or your family but I will if I have to. Show him, Tony," said John. Tony slapped Anna across the face. She cried out in pain but the sound came out as a muffled moan.

"You see Charles, we can hurt you.

But if you cooperate with us fully we will go and you will out come out of this alive and unharmed. I promise you that Charles. We're professionals, not some mad dog hired hands. We're the real deal. But first you have to help us."

"Please. Whatever you want. Just don't hurt my family anymore," whimpered Charles.

"You're a professional too, aren't you Charles. I know you work at the National bank. In fact I know that you're the Head Manager at the National bank."

"Where are you going with this?"

"The safe Charles. I know that the safe is impenetrable. You can't drill through it, you can't saw through it. In fact that son of a bitch could take a tank shell and just sit there saying, "Is that all you got?" The only way in is the time lock or the time lock override. Now that is where you come in. You are the only one who has the time lock override code."

"I won't give it to you."

"Come on Charlie boy. It's just money. All you have to do is give me that seven digit code, I ring my associates and bam! We've got the money, you and your family get away unhurt."

"I could lose my job."

"When they ask questions, you just tell them we tied up and threatened to kill your family. No amount of money or job in the world is worth your family's lives. If your bosses think differently fuck them."

"OK, OK. It's on my computer. I'll get it for you."

"Good man Charlie. Hear that Mike. Your dad's a hero. He just saved your lives."

Mike grunted through the tape.

Something then dawned on John.

"Charles, where is your daughter?"

"I don't have a daughter," said Charles.

"Yes you do. Megan, blonde, seventeen years old, 5 foot 6 inches, Goes to West London College and she plays football on a Wednesday night. I've done my research Charles. Like I said I'm a professional. Now, where the fuck is she?"

"She is out with her football friends."

"At 10pm on a school night?"

"Yes," said Charles.
John smashed Charles' nose with the butt of his gun. Blood squirted out of his face and he clamped his hand over it in an attempt to stem the bleeding.

"Aghh! You broke my nose."

"Charles, that's just the start if you don't work with me. We sat and watched you all come in, none of you left. I know she is here. Now where is she Charles?!"

"I don't know."

"Lads," Tony and Danny pointed their guns at Anna and Mike's heads.

"Charles. Tell me where she is or your family is about to drop by two members. On 3. 1…"

"Ok, ok, ok. Please, please. She is in the basement."

"Why is she in the basement?"
She likes it down there. H-h-h her room is in the basement."

"Really? In a 4 bedroom house your daughter sleeps in the basement?"

"Yes."

"Ok Charlie boy. You're coming with me."

"Where to?"

"The basement. We're gonna go down there and get Megan. Lads, if he comes back without me, shoot them all."

"Ok Boss," said Tony and Danny. John pushed the barrel of his gun into Charles' back and said

"Ok. Show the way please"
They walked into the kitchen and to the door that led to the basement.

"You know we don't have to go down there. She doesn't know you're here. We could just leave her out of this," said Charles.

"No, that doesn't work for me. Just get the fuck down there."
Charles let out a sigh then opened the door and they walked down the stairs. As they reached the bottom John couldn't believe what he was seeing. The room was large and all the walls were covered in sound proofing material. In the corner stood a cage measuring 10 feet by 10 feet. The bars were set into the concrete floor and walls. Lay on a mattress on the floor of the cage and covered with white linen sheets was Megan. A notebook was on the floor just outside the cage with a pen

laid on top of it. Next to it was a glass of water and a half eaten sandwich. She was gasping for breath and unhealthily pale.

"What the fuck is all this!" said John.

"Please, it's not how it looks," said Charles.

"You sick sons o' bitches!"

"No, Please. You don't understand," said Charles.

"I understand just fine! You're keeping your daughter as some kind of sex slave. Did we catch you in the middle of something you sick fuck? Give me the keys!"

"What? No! You got it all wrong!" John punched Charles in the face and knocked him to the floor then pushed the gun against his temple.

"Give me the keys or I'll spread your brains over the floor and take them from you."

Charles hesitated but then passed them to him.

"Now you stay there and be a good doggie. I'm getting her out of here. I'll take her to the police and leave her with a note explaining that her sick family are abusing her."

With that he unlocked the door and walked over to Megan.

"Hey Megan. Hi. I'm John. I'm gonna get you out of here."

He crouched down next to her and lifted her head. Her eyes were bloodshot and half closed.

"Leave me alone," she whispered.

"Please let me help you. I'm not going to hurt you. You're safe now," he said trying to reassure her.

"No, please. You can't be here. It's not safe," she said and grimaced in pain.

John heard the cage door close behind him and realized he had left the keys in the lock. He stood up and turned around.

"What the hell are you doing Charles? You can't go back up there without me."

"I told you, it's not what it looks like."

"Open the door Charles."

"You see she hasn't always been like this."

"Open the fucking door!"

From behind John, Megan let out a scream. He spun round to see her contorting on the floor. Her limbs flexed, bulged and shook. They then began to grow in length.

"She went out with her friends five months ago. She, she was attacked."

"Please open the door, Charles." Megan's screams turned into roars as she got to her feet. Her face was changing, her shoulders jerked backwards, clicked forwards and grew out as the muscles bulged and shifted beneath her skin.

"The police said she was attacked by a big stray dog but the friends were adamant that it was a wolf."
Megan's face began to elongate into a snout as her maxilla and mandibular jaws crunched and grew. Huge teeth pushed out from her gums between her existing teeth. Her cheekbones pushed out from her face and the bones of her skull moved as the gap between her eyes widened. Thick black hair sprouted from her skin and continued to grow until her entire body was completely covered. A thick mane stood around her neck.

"Please Charles. Open the fucking door man!" said John.

His voice in shrill shout. His eyes bulged and sweat was poured from every pore. He had never felt fear like this.

"I told you we should have left her out of this."

The beast stepped towards John. He pointed the gun at her and pulled the trigger. She yelped as the bullet hit her but then grabbed his arm and snapped it. He screamed. She dragged him towards her, buried her huge teeth in his neck and tore his throat out. Blood poured out of him. He coughed and tried to scream, nothing but a weak gurgling came from his mouth. She sunk her teeth into his chest and tore another chunk out of him. His lung was ripped and he was dead by the time she began eating him.

Charles couldn't bear to watch her while she ate. When she had finished he turned to look at his daughter. She was monstrous and she terrified him. Despite all that she was still his daughter. There was not much left of John. Just shoes and some scraps of material.

Charles opened the door and said,

"Now Megan, remember. Like we

have been practicing. Don't attack me, your Mum or your Brother. Only the intruders in the house."

She walked up to him. She towered a foot over him then sniffed the top of his head and nuzzled her snout against the side of his face spreading blood across his cheek. It took everything he had not to pull away or shudder. She walked up the stairs and kicked the door open.

"What was that? Hey Boss is that you?" said Danny.

"Your husband better be playing along and getting your daughter up here. I'm gonna enjoy tying her up," said Tony as he rubbed the barrel of his gun against Anna's cheek and licked his lips.

She let out a muffled cry.

"Tony...er...Tony. What the fuck is that?!" said Danny.

Tony looked up. The beast that was stood in the kitchen doorway stared right at him. She cocked her head to the side.

"Fuck me man. That's one fucking amazing werewolf costume."

Both the men laughed until the werewolf let out a deafening roar and they both stopped laughing. Danny stepped back

78

shaking his head.

"No way man. No fucking way. That can't be real."

"Calm down, Danny. It's Charles in a suit. I'll show you."

He pointed his gun at the wolf but before he could pull the trigger she leapt on him. She grabbed him in her teeth and swung him round by his neck. Danny made a bolt for the stairs. He could hear Tony screaming his name but fear made him keep running. He was at the top of the stairs before he turned back but there was nothing he could do. The wolf was already ripping through Tony's ribs and tearing his chest open like a dog with a rabbit carcass. He turned and ran into one of the bedrooms and slammed the door. He picked up a chair and threw it through the window. A metal shutter came down and blocked his escape route. He cried out then ran his hand back and forth over his head. He ran back out onto the landing and the wolf was at the top of the stairs. She looked at him and bared her blood stained teeth. Pieces of Tony still hung from her jaws. Danny ran into the bathroom and locked the door in the half hope that it would stop a seven foot tall werewolf. He climbed into the bath and sobbed a like child.

Charles watched Megan stomp her way up the stairs. He had already grabbed a pair of scissors from the kitchen. He ran out and cut the tape holding Anna's hands and ankles and then did the same with Mike. He then helped them get free and they ran into the kitchen undoing their gags as they went. They heard the bathroom door being kicked in and the man wailing.

"No! No!" Danny screamed.

Spit flew from between his teeth and his heart beat a furious rhythm against his ribs. The werewolf approached him and there was nothing he could do to stop it. He knew he was going to die and he wet himself. She jumped on him, smashing the bathtub as she rammed his body against it. He pushed the barrel of his gun to his temple and pulled the trigger but any hope of escape via suicide were extinguished as the gun jammed. He screamed till his vocal chords tore as she pulled his chest open and began to eat him.

Downstairs the other members of the Lloyd family ran into the basement. Charles grabbed the mop and bucket on the way. They got into the cage, locked the door then cleaned out the blood and what remained of John. They then huddled together and tried to sleep but it wasn't easy with Megan tearing the house and the furniture apart upstairs. The morning finally came and Megan walked down the stairs in her human form and dressed in her bath robe. Her face and hair were covered in blood

"Oh thank God. I thought I had attacked you, there is so much blood. Are you all ok?" she said.

"Yes," said Charles with a smile.

The Appointment

Douglas Wilson found himself walking into a room. A woman in her late twenties spoke to a tall man who sat behind a desk that was on the other side of the room. He was of medium build with short cropped hair and a short neat beard.

"Mr. Wilson is here to see you. He's your 9.30," she said.

"Ah yes, thank you Lilith. Come in Mr. Wilson. Please have a seat," said the man.

He looked up from a file and gestured towards the chair on the other side of his desk.

Douglas felt like he was waking from dream or at least a daydream. He couldn't remember being in a waiting room though.

He sat down in the seat and looked around the room. It looked like a doctor's office or a car dealer's sales room. All white walls, filing cabinets and general office paraphernalia. The desk was made of pine with stacks of files and a desk tidy. It was filled with pencils, pens, erasers, sharpeners etc.

"Mr. Wilson...Wilson," said the man to himself as he rooted through the files. "Ah yes. Douglas Wilson?"

"Yes," said Douglas with a polite smile that never reached his eyes.

"Mr. Douglas Wilson. Yes, Indeedy, Mr. Douglas Wilson. I've been waiting a long time to see you, Sir," said the man with almost too much zest for Douglas' liking.

"You have? Not to sound lost but..."

"Yes, I mean, it's you. *The* Douglas Wilson," said the man enthusiastically, cutting Douglas off mid-sentence.
He then burst into an apology.

"I'm sorry I'm forgetting my manners. My name is Nick Hobbs."

"Nice to meet you Mr. Hobbs. Sorry I must be having a senior moment. I don't know how I got here," said Douglas.

"Don't worry about that Douglas. We'll get to that. It's just some formalities, just a few forms to fill in," said Nick with a smile.

"Erm… ok."
Nick opened the file with Douglas' name

printed neatly at the top. Inside there was a photo of him paper clipped to a sheet of paper that looked like a patient history file. Nick sifted through the file and took out a few forms. He selected a pen from the desk tidy and started to write on the first form.

"Ok. Douglas Wilson. Male. How old are you Douglas?"

"Fifty Five."

"Fifty...Five. And your profession?"

"I'm the Deputy Manager of Taylor and Lawdson's Sanitation supplies."

"Deput...Tayl....Sani...supplies. Are you married?"

"Yes...well, widowed."

Nick shot Douglas a look of what seemed like false surprise.

"Oh I am sorry to hear that," he said. Douglas Smiled sheepishly and looked down at his feet.

"Children?"

"Erm. No. We. My wife couldn't erm."

"You're sorry about that too," muttered Nick.

"Pardon?" said Douglas.

"I said I'm Sorry about that too."

"No. You said you're."

"When?"

"Just then. You said you're, not I'm."

"I'm sorry but you're mistaken. Can we please get on with this Doug? We need to get it done. Are you a religious man?" Douglas was a bit flustered but answered the question

"Yes. I'm Christian."

"Do you go to church?"

"Yes every Sunday."

"Anything else?"

"Yes, I go to prayer sessions."

"And what do you do there?"

"We pray for people who need God's help in times of need."

"Did you pray for your wife when she was ill?"

"Erm no she committed, erm, suicide."

"So is she beyond God's help now?"

"Some people think that. Self-sin and that."

"Do you pray for yourself, Doug?"

"Yes. Of course I do."

"Do you ever pray for forgiveness?"

"Forgiveness? Forgiveness for what?!"

"You know full well what for," said Nick in a quiet angered tone.

"What is this all about? Where Am I?"

demanded Douglas.

"Let me tell you a story. It's about a woman. A lovely young woman, religious like yourself; though *she* never committed any major sin. All she wanted to do since she was a little girl was be a good wife to a good husband. Even more than that she wanted to be a mum. A Mummy to a little boy or a girl who she could look after and raise. That's all she wanted from life. To see them take their first steps, say their first words. To take them to their first day at school and see them grow up. Later to see them get married and bear her grandchildren. The Maternal Instinct, one of the most important instincts. Makes the mother look after her children so they will grow up big and strong.

So she waited, found a good man, from a good family, with a good job. She could have just gone out and got herself pregnant but she chose to do the right thing and got married. She had never even felt the touch of a man until their wedding day.

He was a good man. Sometimes though, he would get angry and hit her.

He'd always apologise after. Saying he was sorry. Saying it wouldn't happen again. Saying it wasn't the real him. Saying that she had driven him to it. He would make her think that it was her fault so she would end up apologising to him.

You may think that she was stupid to apologise but she loved him. Loved him so completely that she never gave up hoping that he would change… Does any of this sound familiar?"

"No," said Douglas.

"Are you sure?"

"Yes."

"Really? What was her name?"

"I don't know."

"Come on Dougie. You were married to her for twenty years. What was her name?"

"I don't know who you're talking about."

"What was her name Douglas?!" yelled Nick.

"I don't..."

"Her name, tell me, *now*!" hissed Nick, glaring at Douglas with nothing but hate in his eyes.

"Mary. Mary. Her name was Mary," said Douglas in a half sob.

"What else did you used to call her?"

"I don't know what you mean."

"Douglas, what else did you used to call her?"

"I didn't call her anything else."

"What? So you never called her stupid, idiot, retard, slut, bitch, fucking whore?"

Douglas shook his head no as his bottom lip trembled.

"It's all written down here, Douglas. I know you're lying."

Douglas tried to get up from the chair but found he couldn't move.

"Yes Mary," continued Nick. "A wonderful Christian name. Now Mary tried to get pregnant many times with Douglas but alas it was to no avail. So she prayed as hard as she could pray to God to bless her with a child. If He did she would look after the child as if he were the child Jesus himself.

Low and behold three weeks later she was pregnant. She was the happiest woman alive. She rung her husband at work but he just made some half-baked excuse that he wasn't able to talk right now. Everyone else was thrilled to bits for the couple. Their families and friends came round, gave them gifts and said prayers. Everyone was happy, everyone but you. You didn't want this baby. You wished this baby would just fuck off, be still born or be miscarried. So what did you do?"

"Nothing. I didn't do anything. It was an accident," said Douglas.

"Was it?" said Nick.

"Yes," fired back Douglas.

"You're quite sure of that?"

"Yes. We were out in the car, there was an accident and the baby died."

"So you didn't hit Mary before the accident?"

"No."

"You didn't beat her."

"No, not at all."

"Douglas, I know you're lying. I already told you it's all written down here."

"It was a car accident," insisted Douglas.

"You came up with a plan. You didn't want this baby so you decided not to leave it to chance. You'd make this baby go away, so you came home from work one day and when Mary greeted you at the door you punched her in the face cracking her cheekbone. You then punched her three more times knocking her unconscious. Then you kicked that little helpless child, you kicked it whilst it was still in its mother's womb. Fourteen times you kicked your unconscious wife in the belly. Fourteen! But that wasn't enough for you so you rolled her onto her back took off your shoes and stamped eight times on the lower abdomen. You carried her to your car put her in the passenger seat and drove onto a dual carriageway. You'd seen a few crash report TV programs, you knew about skid marks on the road. So you got up to seventy miles per hour then broke hard and slammed your car passenger side first into the crash barriers at forty miles per hour. Your story about a youth running across the carriageway convinced the police. Mary was in a critical condition for two weeks. She lost the baby but not only that, her abdominal injuries were so severe that she had to have an emergency hysterectomy taking away her ability to have another baby. You had stolen the one thing from her that she wanted most in life. That's what happened isn't it."

"How can you know all this? Mary never told the police."

"We're not with the police, Doug. That's what happened isn't it?"

"Yes," said Douglas looking at the floor.

"You murdered her that day," said Nick.

"*What*?"

"You murdered her."

"I didn't murder my wife."

"Yes you did," said Nick nodding his head.

"No, she committed suicide twelve years later."

"And why did she do that?"

"I don't know because she was crazy. I didn't know it would affect her like that."

"Oh please. Douglas, you might be able to bullshit yourself but don't bullshit me."

"After that accident she was devastated. I didn't know she wanted a baby that much. She never touched me anymore, she just sat and cried. She wouldn't talk to me, she would never clean the house. She needed to be sorted out, to be disciplined..."

"So you decided to discipline her by beating her to a pulp and raping her at least once a week?" cut in Nick.

"No."

"You knocked out six of her teeth. You punched her so hard one time the retina detached in her left eye. You broke her nose, slashed her with razor blades, and put cigarettes out on the soles of her feet while she was asleep."

"Ok. I did things, bad things, but I didn't murder her."

"Do you think she would have killed herself if you hadn't killed her baby? Do you think she would have killed herself if you hadn't injured her so badly that she couldn't have any more babies? Do you think she would have killed herself if you hadn't tortured and raped her for twenty years?" the words hissed through Nick's teeth.

"No," said Douglas, shaking his head.

"If you hadn't done all those things to her she would still be happy, she would still be alive today with children; your children. But you Douglas, you're a sadistic little fuck. A shit stain of a man. In fact I wouldn't even call you a human. You're a vulgar, little, horrible wretch. Because of what you did she killed herself. She killed herself because of what you did. Because of you Douglas. Because of you!"

"Please. Where am I? What are you doing this for?" cried Douglas.
The room fell silent. Nick stared at Douglas for a whole minute…
He then broke the silence.

"That train must have really hit you hard" he said coldly.

"What train? What are you talking about?"

"You were in your car before you got here. You decided to cross the level crossing as the gates were closing. You didn't realise that the train was only fifty feet away doing eighty miles an hour. You didn't stand a chance."
The memories slowly came back to Douglas. The train slamming into his car, the moment of horrendous pain, then everything fading into white and

walking into this office.

"I'm...I'm...I'm dead?" said Douglas.

"Yes" said Nick with a sly smile. "A pathetic end to a pathetic little fuck."

"What's going to happen to me? Am I going to Heaven?" asked Douglas.
Nick Laughed, mocking him.

"Have you even listened to anything that I've just said?"
Something dawned on Douglas. He was remembering names from the bible. The names given to Demons.

"Oh God, please help me!"

"A little too late to repent now, Dougie boy."

"Lilith, the first woman in the Garden of Eden who God cast out. Nick, Old Nick, Lucifer. Hobbs, Devils."
Nick smiled at Douglas, a smile that chilled him to his core.

"Am I in hell?" said Douglas. His voice failing.

"Hmm. Depends on how you look at it."

"What does that mean?"

"Let's go over a few things. God made everything."

"In seven days, yes."

"Shut up when you're being told the truth, Douglas. God made everything, yes. He made the earth in seven days. Everything else took a bit longer. He had already made Heaven, he made the Angels to do his bidding, no questions asked. He made animals. Then he made humans. He decided to give them free will, and what did *you* do? You took that free will literally and you ran around doing whatever the fuck you liked. Most humans are good, peaceful people. Then you get ones like you. Bad people. Now God takes his time making people but he can only do so much because of the free will. He puts the soul into the foetus at an early stage and sends it on its way. Now, because he takes time doing this he gets angry when a person is destroyed purposefully by another; extremely angry. I asked you if you pray for forgiveness because most people do. Usually for little things, they swore, they stole something small. They had what they see as bad thoughts: Revenge, sexual, or greed. They looked at porn, that sort of thing. So God is lenient and forgives them. But you see, forgiveness doesn't work quite the way you have been taught. Or at least the way *you* seem to think it does. When you have killed your family you can't just go into a church and repent or confess. Say a few hail Mary's and everything is ok. If you, Douglas, want God's forgiveness you're going to have to earn God's forgiveness. *Really* fucking earn it. It comes at a price though. A rather hefty price."

"What is the price?" whisper Douglas. Nick looked down at his desk and when he looked back up the chilling smile was back on his face.

"You really want to know?"

"Yes."

"He wants back what he gave you."

"What's that?"

"The thing that he gave you."

"What thing?" said Douglas getting irate.

"Your soul."

"My Soul?"

"Yes."

"Then he can have it. Please, he can have it."

"Not that easy Dougie. The people of

your modern human society would tell you that this is Hell. That this is the place that Satan or Lucifer had created after he fell, but it was God that made this place. Yes, Lucifer was the manager for a while but he wasn't and still isn't a Demon. God made this place and he made all the things in it. The point is souls are difficult to make. They are even more difficult to destroy. To forgive *your* sins your soul must be destroyed. God has given me the permission to absolve you of yours."

"You're going to absolve me of my...You're going to destroy my soul?

"Yes."

"If you do these things to people. What makes you different from me?" said Douglas trying to be cocky.

"God made me, I'm just doing his bidding. I can't question him. Whereas you, you had free will. You could have treated Mary with love and respect as you should have done. Instead you did what you did and because of your actions Mary died, your baby died." Douglas broke down and wept.

"What's going to happen to me?" he

said.

"The first real emotion you show is in sympathy for yourself? You disgust me! You will be taken from here and your punishment will be issued."

"What is my punishment? How long will it last?" whimpered Douglas.

"Centuries, Millennia. Hard to say. I won't be happy until your head is nothing more than a screaming, bloody skull stripped of all its flesh," said Nick. Douglas wailed and sobbed. He shook as fear coursed through his body.

"Hetron, Serfek. He's ready for you!" called Nick.
Two well-built men came into the room and stood on either side of Douglas. Nick leaned forwards in his chair looked Douglas right in the eye and said,

"I don't like you. I hate…no, in fact hate isn't a strong enough word for how I feel about you. Your presence here in my room sickens me. I abhor your entire existence. But you know what, Douglas Wilson? In here I'm the closest thing you have to a friend. These two men might look tough but the way they look shows nothing of what they are capable of, kind

of like you. Take him out of my sight!"
The two men grabbed Douglas the
shoulders then dragged him out of the
room kicking and screaming.

"No! Please! Noooo!"

"Next" shouted Nick to Lilith.

THREE WISHES

I had found this little item in an antiques shop. It looked just like the lamp depicted in books and films about Aladdin and the Genie which I had enjoyed as a child. As I picked it up I found it to be a lot heavier than I had expected. It was also heavily tarnished and had seen better days but I liked it as it had a certain 'charm' to it. I thought it would look nice as a talking point in my new flat.

"How much for this?" I said to the shop owner.

From his chair behind the till he lowered the newspaper just enough to see the lamp. He then raised his eyes to look at me.

"Five quid, mate," he said.

His Turkish accent was laced with a cockney twang.

I paid him and went on my way.

The lamp sat on my living room coffee table for two months. It drew the attention from my friends and family that I had hoped it would.

One day I looked at it and noticed some writing on the side so I tried to clean it up a bit. I held it in one hand and gave it a rub using the edge of my t-shirt with the other. Thick, black smoke began to pour from the spout of the lamp and in my surprise I dropped the thing. It hit the ground and the smoke continued to flow from the object. The smoke began to take the form of a semi-solid humanoid figure. It was six feet tall, as black as coal and had no facial features except for two glowing red eyes.

It's fair to say that at this point I was scared out of my wits and fear held me on the spot even though my mind screamed at me to run.

Those eyes stared right into me like it could see my soul. It then spoke in a voice that made the room shake.

"I am the Jinn, DenGhall. You have freed me from my Earth bound tomb. As reward I grant you three wishes. Use them as you will but be wise about the choices you make. There may be consequences attached to that which you ask for."

In those days I was young and a fool. I

could have thought about what to ask for but instead I rushed into it and said the first things that came into my head.

"I want to live forever. And...and I want to be indestructible. I want to be rich too," I said.

See, I did say I was a fool.

"Your wishes are granted and I am freed from the bonds which for so long have held me in this dimension."

The smoke dissipated and once again I was alone in my living room.

In my excitement I rushed out to the nearest ATM to my house and checked my balance. After I had typed in my pin and pressed the correct buttons the screen displayed the amount of '£500,000,000' in my account.

My phone began to ring. 'Bank' read the name on my phones screen. I answered it and my bank manager spoke.

"Hello Mr. Jones. How are you today? I see you have come into some money. Would you like to come in so we can discuss your accounts with us?"

"I can't right now, I have too many things to do," I said.

I hung up the phone and then rung my

bosses phone number.

"Hi Dennis. Seth Jones here. I'm just ringing to tell you I quit with immediate effect," I said.

"You can't do that!" he said.

"Watch me," I said and laughed as I hung up the phone.

Over the next few years I bought a big house, took all my friends and family on holiday and had a lot of fun.

I used to find it funny to do crazy things and not get hurt. I would do them just to see people's reactions.

I found fame after I jumped out of a plane and 'accidentally' forgot to pull the ripcord on my parachute but survived the fall without a scratch. People screamed as I hit the floor but then I just picked myself up and dusted myself off.

I set the record for the longest, deepest ocean dive without an oxygen tank. People paid a lot of money to shoot guns at me, only to see the bullets flatten themselves against my skin.

I had to turn down one man's offer of millions to play Russian roulette against him, you can imagine how that would have ended.

The years rolled by, then I met and married my girlfriend, Sadi. We had three children together, none of whom inherited my 'abilities'.

I began to realise how big a mistake I had made when my family and friends grew older but, despite the passing years, I remained the same age.

Life isn't much fun when you have to watch the people you love die around you. First my wife, then my children, then my grandchildren and then my great grandchildren.

After many years I had outlived so many generations of my family that I had to acknowledge I had no place with my descendants anymore, so I moved on. I would drift from place to place. I could never stay anywhere longer than ten years as every person I would befriend would eventually grow old and die.

I began to lose track of time. Years turned into decades and the decades into centuries. Sometimes I would sleep for years, not because I was tired but because I was bored. New things came and went but eventually nothing could impress me anymore.

I was shocked the first time I noticed that a millennium had passed. The years just kept on going, flashing by like shooting stars.

The severity of my wishes took a horrific new twist when the human race began to die out. Not just a few in extreme places but cities full of people on every continent. Humans took over two hundred fifty thousand years to reach twenty billion people, and just seventy five years to become almost entirely extinct as a species. All except one, me, although I'm not really sure if I can be classed as a human anymore. The plague that wiped them out had no effect on me. I cried for decades. The loneliness I felt ate at my soul and at my humanity.

Other species took their turn to advance and fill the void that humans left. Some of them were successful too but inevitably they came and went just like the humans.

It was because the earth had started to warm up. It's got to a level where eventually it has become a hostile, uninhabitable planet. The oceans evaporated and along the equator the ground is so hot that it is semi-solid.

I sit here now on top of a mountain. It doesn't have a name. I am the only living thing left on the entire planet and I have never named it. It was formed when the tectonic plates began to crash into each other in the middle of the Pacific Ocean; when there was still an ocean.

I lost count a long time ago of how many years it has been since I made those wishes. I assume though it is somewhere around six billion years. I read an article once which said that is how long it would take the sun to go supernova, and here I am watching the sun. It is ten times the size it was when I was young. Soon it will collapse in on itself and send out a shockwave that will destroy the entire solar system.

Hopefully it will destroy me along with it. I would say that I wish for death, but I have become extremely careful about what I wish for.

Author Bio

I am Paul James Kearns. I come from Bolton, a town in the North West of England. I have lived here all my life. I am engaged to Carrie and have two children. When I was young I was deemed by some teachers as 'a bit of a slow learner'. This was because when it came to writing I couldn't keep up with my classmates. I now think that I have mild dyslexia.

My mum would encourage me to write short stories to improve my writing skills. Needless to say I don't think the teachers could have realised the monster they inadvertently created.

I don't like to be told I can't do things. I'm also not one to give up easily on something that I have decided I'm going to see through to the end. Hence I never stopped writing. I had one teacher at Little Lever Secondary School called Mr. Roberts. He taught English. He must have seen some spark of creativity in me. He always encouraged me to write sci-fi stories when we had a writing project. If perchance you are reading this

Mr. Roberts, Thank you. You have had a huge influence on my life.

To you the reader. Thank you for buying this book. Seriously without you I am just a man writing down his crazy ideas.

This book is a collection of stories that have been bashed around in my brain. Put down into written word and then refined and edited into what you hold in your hands. The stories are all for entertainment purposes only. They may have given you chills, thrills and even scares. They may stay with you long after you have closed this book. Essentially though, I hope you enjoyed reading them as much as I did writing them. Maybe they have given you a bit of inspiration to write your own stories too. Thank you and happy reading.

My website is:
Pauljkearnsauthor.wixsite.com/twistedtales

You can also find me on facebook as:
@PJKearnsAuthor

Twitter as:
@pjkearnsauthor

Wordpress as:
Pauljkearnsauthor.wordpress.com

Instagram as: pauljkearnsauthor

Other books by Paul J Kearns:
Soldiers of the S.O.V.E.U.

Printed in Great Britain
by Amazon

77200793R00070